Not Quite Snow White

written by **Ashley Franklin** • illustrated by **Ebony Glenn**

HARPER
An Imprint of HarperCollinsPublishers

Not Quite Snow White
Text copyright © 2019 by Ashley Franklin
Illustrations copyright © 2019 by Ebony Glenn
All rights reserved. Manufactured in China.

For information address HarperCollins Children's Books, a division of HarperCollins Publishers,
195 Broadway, New York, NY 10007.
www.harpercollinschildrens.com
ISBN 978-0-06-279860-2
The artist used Adobe Photoshop to create the digital illustrations for this book.
Typography by Jeanne Hogle
19 20 21 22 23 SCP 10 9 8 7 6 5 4 3 2 1
❖
First Edition

To Mom Mom, the queen who taught this princess that
a golden heart is worth more than a silver spoon
—A. F.

For every girl who dares to dream
—E. G.

For Tameika, it was always the right time and place to dance and sing.

Tameika had a hip-rolling happy dance.

A swayful sad dance.

A stomping mad dance.

And a hair-flicking just-because-she-felt-fabulous dance.

She sang high with the tweeting birds and low with the croaking frogs. She always shared her love of music and movement with an audience (stuffed and unstuffed).

Tameika loved the stage. It was her perfect place. She was the star of every show, and she loved every show that she starred in.

She had been a cucumber,

a space cowgirl,

a dinosaur,

and—her favorite part—a singing mermaid.

Onstage, Tameika felt like she could be anything or anyone she wanted to be, but she had never been a princess. Now she would finally have her chance.

Tameika was so excited that she went to both days of auditions for the Snow White musical. On the first day, she arrived super early.

She helped friends with their lines, kept count for the dancers, and shooed butterflies from nervous tummies so songs could be sung.

After the audition, Tameika heard some of the other kids whispering.

"She can't be Snow White."   "She's too tall!"   "She's much too chubby."

"And she's too brown."

Tameika looked at her legs. They were long. Maybe the kids were right. A princess shouldn't be taller than her prince. Should she?

She looked at her belly. Maybe what the kids said was true. She could not remember any chubby princesses.

Tameika looked at her skin. She was brown. How could a girl with brown skin play a princess like Snow White?

Could those kids be wrong?
Maybe she was wrong for
wanting to be this princess.

Tameika slouched and sucked in her belly. She tried pulling down her sleeves. But there was no getting around being brown.

For the first time, she didn't feel like dancing or singing.

At dinner, Tameika didn't tap her feet
or clang rhythms with her spoon.

"Is something wrong?" asked her mom.
"The other kids said I'm too tall, too chubby, and too brown.
I'm not right for Snow White," said Tameika.

"You've got it all wrong," Mom said. "You are tall enough,
chubby enough, and brown enough to be a perfect princess."

"Besides," said her dad, "Snow White is just pretend. You've always been my real princess.

"You're just enough of all the right stuff." He kissed her forehead.

Tameika smiled. Maybe her parents were on to something.

At the audition the next day, Tameika
watched all the other kids get onstage
and do their best.

SNOW
WHITE
The Musical

AUDITIONS
TODAY!

It was Tameika's turn at last. She remembered what her parents had said, but her long legs were still a little jittery.

She closed her eyes and imagined she was singing and dancing for her favorite audience of friends (stuffed and unstuffed).

Then she remembered the joy she felt when performing. Tameika knew she could do it.

And she did!
She shone like the
star she was.

She could act. She could dance. She could sing. She loved herself as much as she loved music and movement.

Tameika was a perfectly poised princess.

When her audition was over, Tameika looked out to smiling faces.
Tameika wasn't too much of anything.

SNOW WHITE
MUSICAL
AUDITIONS
TODAY!

Maybe she was just enough of all the right stuff.